KiNG BEN and SiR RHINO

Eric Sailer

Two Lions?
Who is the *other* lion?

two lions

To the real King Ben

Text and illustrations copyright © 2018 by Eric Sailer

Published by Two Lions, New York
www.apub.com

Amazon, the Amazon logo, and Two Lions are trademarks of Amazon.com, Inc., or its affiliates.

ISBN-13: 9781503939844
ISBN-10: 1503939847

The illustrations were rendered in ink, watercolor, and gouache.
Book design by Tanya Ross-Hughes

Printed in China
First edition
10 9 8 7 6 5 4 3 2 1

Ben was king of the jungle.
He ruled over all the land.

He had everything
a king could want:
castles,

noble steeds,

and **servants**!

Indeed, Ben had everything except . . .

... a loyal subject.

Hey,
play with me!!!

For no local peasant
heeded his authority until he met . . .

Ben rejoiced by performing
the royal ceremonies.

Then **fun** was proclaimed.

First, Ben declared games.

He issued snacks.

He decreed

mayhem!

LRAOW RRAOW RRAOW EOWW!

Then he spotted new riches to add to his collection.

After all,
a king
can **have**
what he
wants.

But trouble
stirred
in the
kingdom. . . . .

Chaos erupted!

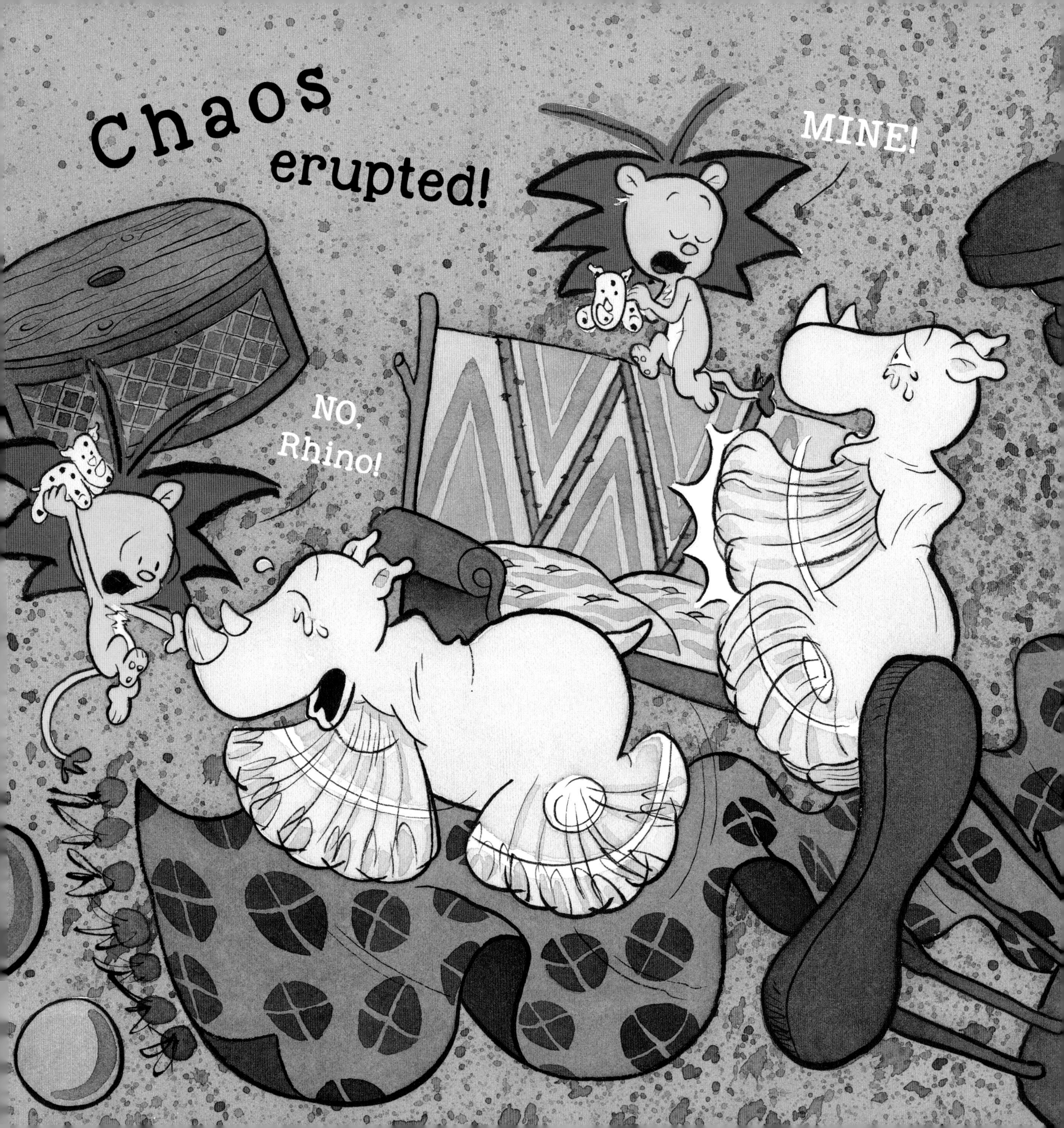

RIP!

And **catastrophe** struck!

It ripped the kingdom apart.

WRARARARARAWR!

Now Ben's court was empty
(except for his servants).

Ben missed his loyal subject . . .
his favorite subject.

So he set out on a quest.

He presented Rhino
with a royal gift.

Will you still play with me?

A **joyous celebration** followed.

Now Ben knows
that to be
a **great** king
of the jungle . . .

HE-OW!

. . . he must be
a **great** friend.